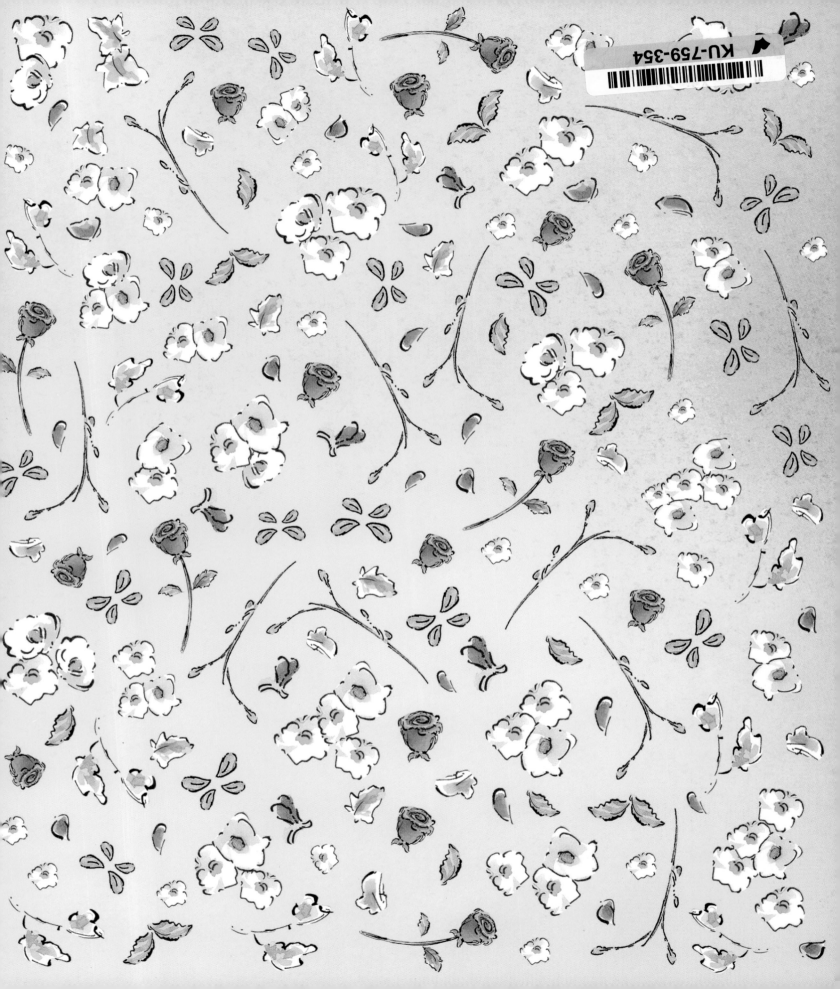

For Judi Hudson – J.W.

First published in Great Britain in 2022 by Andersen Press Ltd.,
20 Vauxhall Bridge Road, London, SW1V 2SA, UK
Vijverlaan 48, 3062 HL Rotterdam, Nederland
Text copyright © Jeanne Willis, 2022.
Illustration copyright © Susan Varley, 2022.
The rights of Jeanne Willis and Susan Varley to be identified
as the author and illustrator of this work
have been asserted by them in accordance with the
Copyright, Designs and Patents Act, 1988.
All rights reserved.
Printed and bound in China.

1 3 5 7 9 10 8 6 4 2

British Library Cataloguing in Publication Data available.
Hardback ISBN 978 1 78344 984 2
Paperback ISBN 978 1 78344 985 9

Marry me, Mole?

Jeanne Willis

Susan Varley

ANDERSEN PRESS

"Mole, why won't you marry me?"

Sang a lonely bird in the maple tree.

"I'll make you the best nest in the sky."

But Mole said...

"NO!"

And Bird said, "Why?

Don't you like my singing?

Don't you like my tree?"

And Mole said...

"Yes! But our love cannot be."

"How," said Bird, "can it not be?
When I love you and you love me?
Let's fly away and start anew."

But Mole said...

"No, it just won't do."

"Or perhaps you just don't care!"
Called Bird from high up in the air.

"Am I too big? Too small? Too old?
Am I too shy? Too young? Too bold?

Am I too slow? Am I too fast?"

But Mole just said...

"Our love won't last."

"It will!" said Bird. "It will unless...
You think my feathers are a mess
And wish I wasn't brown but blue?"
And Mole said...

"No, that isn't true!
I'm fond of brown, your feathers shine!"

"Then why," said Bird, "won't you be mine
And live beside me in the sun?"
And Mole said...

"It just can't be done!

I live below, you live above."

"So?" cried Bird. "We are in love!

Love's what makes the world go round...

I'll move in with you, underground.

We'll make it work, we'll have a lark..."

And down he went into the dark.

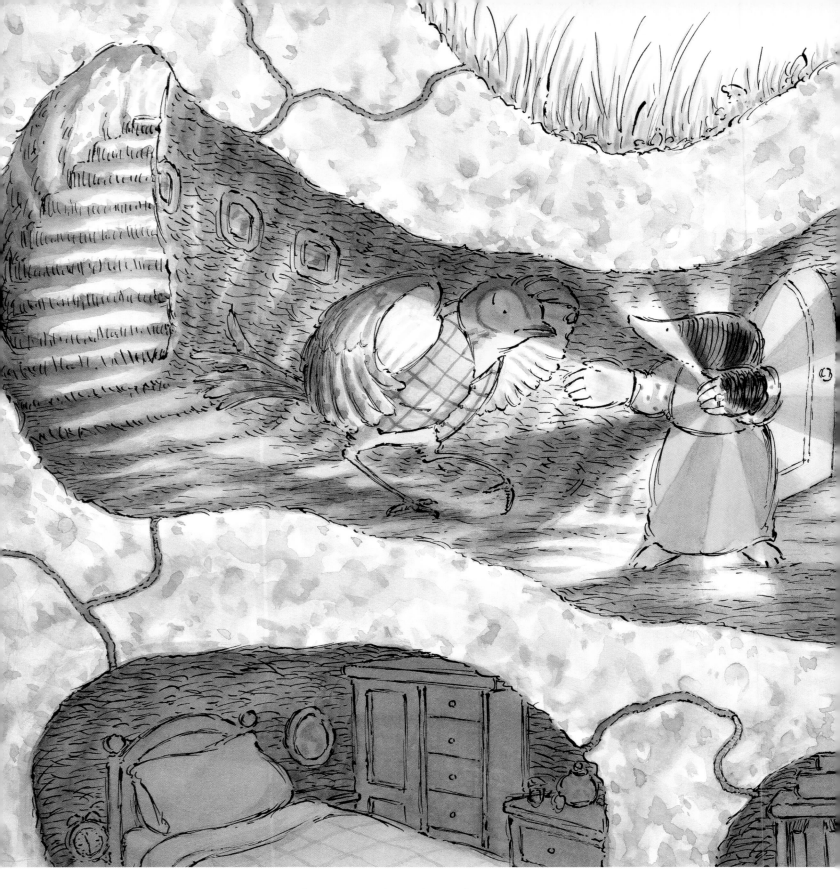

Down the tunnel in the gloom,

He could not spread his wings - no room!

He could not see a single thing
Except for Mole's engagement ring.

"Perhaps," he said, "it would be best

If you lived with me in my nest

Instead of underneath this hill,

The lack of sunshine makes me ill."

But Mole said...

"Sorry, I can't fly."

"Oh no!" cried Bird. "Is this goodbye?"

"I'll always love you, Bird," said Mole,
"But I belong inside a hole
And you belong up in the sky."
"You're right," said Bird and gave a sigh.

"You love the night...

I love the day.

We cannot live our lives that way,
And though it breaks my heart to leave
It's for the best, I do believe."
And Mole said...

"Sometimes, life is tough.

Sometimes, love is not enough.

But out there somewhere there will be...

Someone for you...

Someone for me."

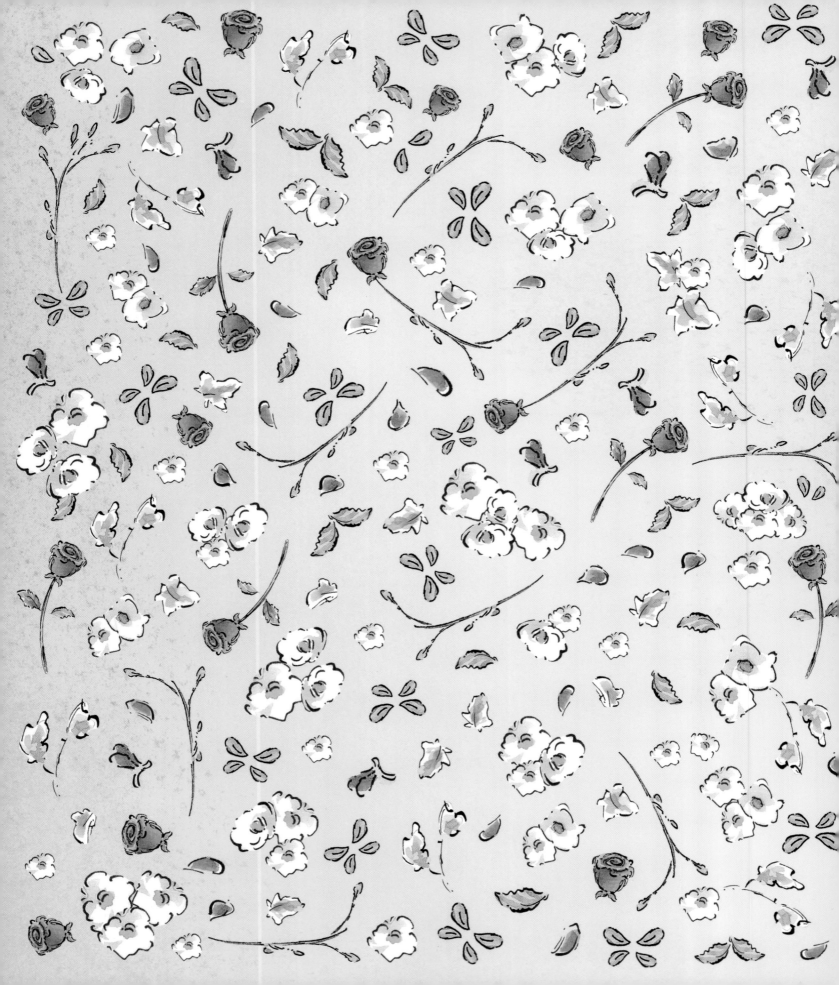

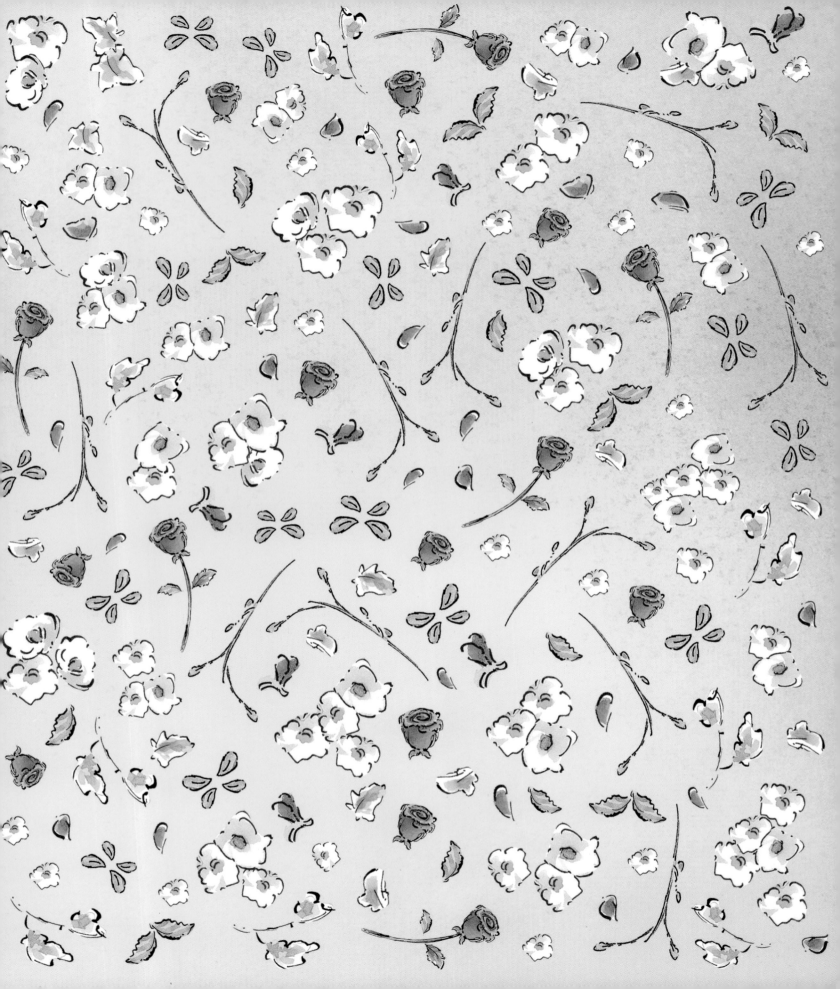